Licensed exclusively to Top That Publishing Ltd
Tide Mill Way, Woodbridge, Suffolk, IP12 1AP, UK
www.topthatpublishing.com
Copyright © 2017 Tide Mill Media
All rights reserved
2 4 6 8 9 7 5 3 1
Manufactured in China

Written by Susie Linn
Illustrated by Edyta Kraczkowska

ISBN 978-1-78700-389-7

A catalogue record for this book is available from the British Library

The Superhero Princess
& Pickle the Wonder Dog

Written by Susie Linn

Illustrated by Edyta Kraczkowska

'Dull, dull, dull!' cried Princess Sophy.
She was bored with everyday
princess duties.

Riding around in a carriage was boring.
Waving at crowds was boring.
Kissing babies was boring.

Princess Sophy looked down at
her dog, Pickle. It was time they
did something exciting!

Luckily, Princess Sophy had a very special secret.
Back in her bedroom, when no one was looking,
she changed from bored princess …

… into Superprincess!

'Come on Pickle,' she said. 'I'm going on an adventure – and you're coming too!' Pickle groaned. He didn't like adventures!

So Superprincess went in search
of superhero things to do.

First, she spotted a cat stuck up a tree.

Meow!
Meow!

'To the rescue!' shouted
Superprincess excitedly.

'Oh, NO!'
groaned Pickle.

Next, Superprincess spotted an old lady who was in danger.

'To the rescue!' she shouted.

'Oh, NO!' groaned Pickle.

It wasn't long before Superprincess was bored again.
'Dull, dull, dull!' she cried. 'Come on Pickle!
Let's find some more exciting things to do!'

Just then, she spotted a bus full
of passengers stuck in some roadworks.
'To the rescue!' she shouted again.

'But we're going the wrong way!'
cried all the passengers, as Superprincess put
their bus down facing in the wrong direction.

'Oh, NO!' groaned Pickle as they zoomed away from the trouble they had made.

As they whizzed around a corner, Superprincess and Pickle almost bumped into three robbers running out of the bank.

'To the rescue!'

'Oh, NO!'

Superprincess took a big roll of ribbon from her cape.
(Even superhero princesses like pretty things!)

Then she flew round and round
the robbers, tying them in one
enormous ribbony bundle,
before leaving them outside
the police station.

Soon, Superprincess was bored again. 'Dull, dull, dull!' she moaned. Pickle just covered his eyes and whimpered.

Superprincess did a deep-sea dive to rescue a broken submarine.

She went to a rainforest to rescue some lost explorers.

She flew to the North Pole to rescue a ship trapped between two icebergs.

She even managed to push a stuck train out of a very, very long tunnel!

Superprincess and Pickle
were just about to go back
to the palace for supper when
Superprincess's phone rang.

'What's that you say?'
she shouted. 'A space
rocket has flown off course?'

'Oh, NO!' groaned Pickle.

'To the rescue!'
cried Superprincess.

When the job was done, and they
were zooming back to Earth
at a zillion miles an hour,
Pickle knew he had
to do something.

Back on the ground, while Superprincess was busy dusting down her cape and adjusting her tiara, Pickle sneaked her phone out of her cape pocket. Then he started to tap a message to the King and Queen.

At last, Superprincess and Pickle arrived back at the palace and changed clothes just in time for supper.

'I hear you've been doing lots of dangerous things!' said the Queen.

'No more adventures for you!' said the King.

'You're grounded!' they both said together.

Even superheroes have to do what their mummy
and daddy say, so Princess Sophy was banned
from going on any more superhero adventures.
But no one said anything about Pickle.

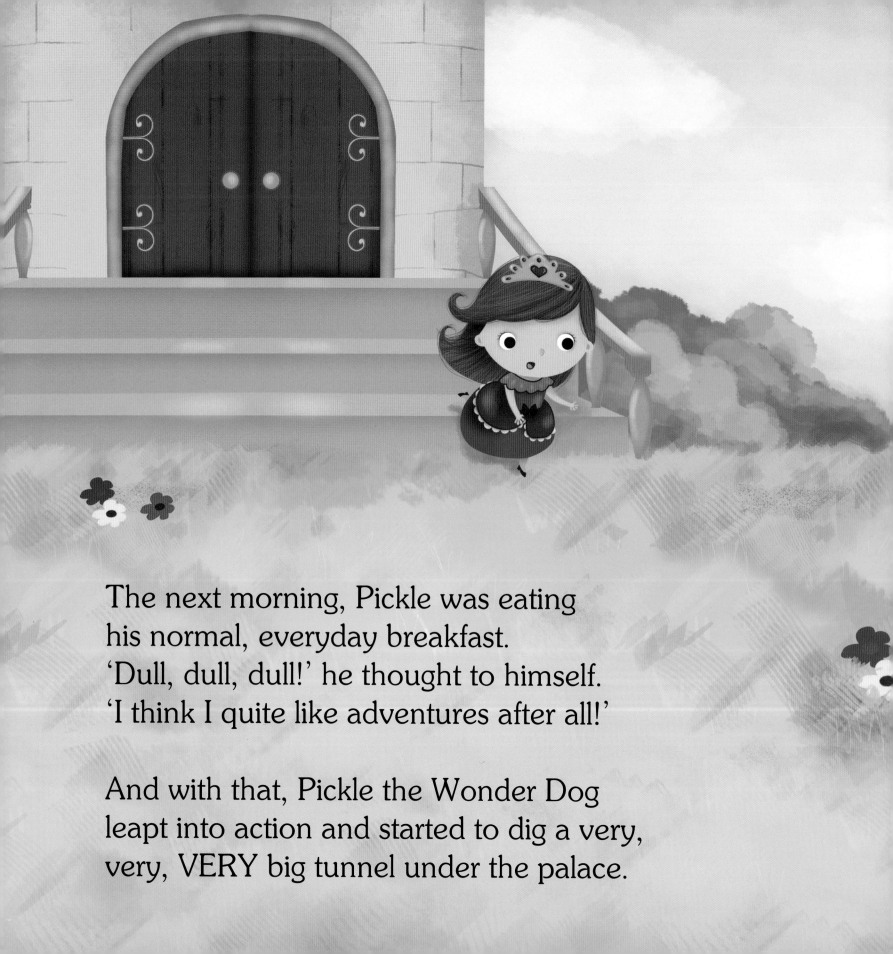

The next morning, Pickle was eating
his normal, everyday breakfast.
'Dull, dull, dull!' he thought to himself.
'I think I quite like adventures after all!'

And with that, Pickle the Wonder Dog
leapt into action and started to dig a very,
very, VERY big tunnel under the palace.

'Oh, NO!' cried Princess Sophy.